DISNEP
PRINCESS

Just Like a Princess

 publications international, ltd.

Illustrated by the Disney Storybook Artists

Published by Louis Weber, C.E.O., Publications International, Ltd.
7373 North Cicero Avenue, Lincolnwood, Illinois 60712

Ground Floor, 59 Gloucester Place, London W1U 8JJ

Customer Service: 1-800-595-8484 or customer_service@pilbooks.com

www.pilbooks.com

p i kids is a registered trademark of Publications International, Ltd.

8 7 6 5 4 3 2 1

Manufactured in China.

ISBN-13: 978-1-4508-0731-9
ISBN-10: 1-4508-0731-3

A Tale of Love

In the middle of the ocean, far beneath the surface of the water, King Triton proudly watched his daughters perform a concert. Tonight's performance was a special show composed by Sebastian the crab. It began with six of King Triton's daughters singing together. At just the right moment, a clamshell would open to reveal the king's youngest daughter, Ariel.

Ariel had the most beautiful voice in all the kingdom. When it was her turn to sing, the audience held its breath in excitement.

"Introducing our seventh little sister," sang the mermaids proudly.

The audience leaned in closer to get a better look. But the clamshell was empty! King Triton gasped. Where in the deep blue sea was Ariel?

Ariel was off with her friend Flounder, exploring a sunken ship. She liked the human world. Ariel wanted human treasures such as cups, saucers, forks, and candlesticks. But what she wanted most of all was to have legs instead of a tail.

One day, a ship floated through the waters above her. Ariel raced to the surface. The minute she laid eyes on handsome Prince Eric, Ariel knew she was in love.

Suddenly, a storm moved in and began to toss the ship. Prince Eric and the sailors tried to fight the waves, but the storm was too much. Eric was thrown into the sea. The waves crashed over him, and he went under!

"I must rescue him!" Ariel said.

Ariel pulled Eric safely to shore. On the beach, she sang a beautiful song to him.

Just as Eric awoke, Ariel slipped into the ocean to swim back home. She wanted to stay and talk to him, but she could not let him see that she was a mermaid. Ariel was just relieved that Eric was all right.

Just then, Flounder swam up to Ariel. "I have a surprise for you," he said. "Come see!"

Flounder showed Ariel a special treasure he had found in the wreckage of the newly sunken ship. It was a statue of Prince Eric.

Ariel was so excited that she swam circles around it.

"I need to be human!" she told her friend.

Suddenly, King Triton arrived. He took one look at Ariel's treasures from the human world and became very angry.

King Triton loved his daughters and wanted them all to be happy, but he worried that the human world was dangerous.

"It's not safe!" King Triton said.

"But …," Ariel stammered.

"Have you lost your senses?" King Triton thundered. "He's a human; you're a mermaid! Ariel, I am going to get through to you. And if this is the only way … so be it!"

And with a wave of his golden triton, Ariel's father destroyed all of her treasures.

Ariel was devastated.

Not far away, the wicked sea witch Ursula was watching Ariel. Ursula wanted to steal King Triton's power, so she devised an evil plan.

"If you give me your voice," Ursula said to Ariel, "I will make you human for three days."

Then Ursula warned Ariel that if Prince Eric did not give her a kiss of true love within those three days, she would turn back into a mermaid and be forced to serve Ursula.

Ariel agreed and began to sing a beautiful song. Ursula captured her voice in a golden shell.

Then Ariel was transformed. She swam through the water with two legs instead of a tail.

Up on land, Prince Eric sat by the seashore and dreamed of the woman who had rescued him.

Suddenly, Prince Eric's dog Max began to bark. He had spotted Ariel by the rocks. Prince Eric ran to Ariel. Could she be the mysterious woman with the beautiful voice who had saved him? Eric was excited to hear her speak, but Ariel could not.

Eric showed Ariel around his kingdom. They laughed and danced and had a wonderful time. Before long, he fell in love with her.

The evil Ursula was watching Eric and Ariel, and she could see that they were indeed in love. Ursula disguised herself as a maiden, and wore the shell that held Ariel's voice around her neck.

Ursula used Ariel's voice to trick Prince Eric. He thought Ursula was the one who had rescued him, so he planned to marry her that very day.

Ariel could not speak, but with the help of Sebastian, Flounder, her other sea friends, and Prince Eric, she fought the wicked Ursula and got her voice back. But she was a mermaid again!

King Triton was overjoyed to have his daughter back safe and sound, but he knew that only one thing would make her happy — love! He cast a magic spell over Ariel, giving her legs once again.

Ariel and Eric, surrounded by their loved ones, were married that very day!

Ariel: A Tale of Love

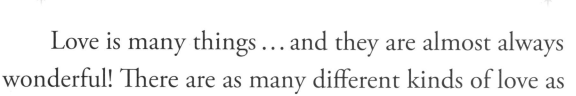

Love is many things … and they are almost always wonderful! There are as many different kinds of love as there are ways to express it.

Love may mean caring about someone so much that you want what is best for them. King Triton loved Ariel. He wanted her to be safe and happy, even if that meant not having her live under the sea.

Ariel loved Eric so much that she was willing to give up something very special so that she could be with him.

Love is very powerful and very important. It is something everyone needs. Sometimes love is hard to describe … but it is impossible to ignore!

A Tale of Kindness

Many years ago in a tiny country town, there lived a young woman named Belle. She was the daughter of a man who invented things, and he taught her to read and to write and to think for herself. Belle was very pretty, very kind, and very, very smart.

Because she was so interested in books, Belle was considered odd by the townspeople. But, because she was so pretty, one man named Gaston thought she would make a good wife. Gaston wanted a wife as pretty as he was handsome.

Belle was not interested in Gaston. She was interested in the lives she read about in her books.

One day Belle's father set off to take his newest invention to the fair. When he did not return, Belle went to search for him.

In the woods, Belle came upon a castle she had never seen before. By the gate, she saw her father's hat. She knocked on the door. When no one answered, she pushed the door open.

"Father!" Belle called out. "Are you here?"

Searching the castle, she found her father locked in a room. "I must get you out of here!"

"You will do no such thing!" roared a terrible voice. Belle looked up and saw a huge beast in the shadows of the hallway.

"Please let my father go free," Belle said. "I will stay in his place."

The Beast freed Belle's father. Belle stayed with the Beast at the castle.

"You may go anywhere you like, except the West Wing," growled the Beast.

Belle soon realized that the Beast's castle was enchanted. She wandered into the kitchen and found the food preparing itself! Mrs. Potts, the teapot, introduced herself. Lumiere, the kind candelabrum, directed the dance of the dishes.

Belle's spirits were lifted by the show put on by her new enchanted friends. She was grateful for their kindness. For the first time since coming to the castle, Belle felt happy.

After eating, Belle decided to explore the castle. She went up a staircase she had not seen before. She did not realize that it led to the West Wing.

Belle was sad to find that this part of the castle was dark and dirty. Most of the furniture was tipped over or broken.

Belle walked to an old table. On it, there was a glowing rose inside a bell jar. Just as she was about to touch it, the Beast stormed into the room.

"Stay away from here," he roared.

Belle raced out of the castle. Even though the castle was intriguing, she could not bear to stay a minute longer with the Beast.

Suddenly, a pack of wolves surrounded her. The Beast pounced and scared the wolves away. Belle was safe, but the Beast was badly hurt.

Belle rushed to the Beast. She carefully helped him back to the castle.

The Beast was very grateful for Belle's help. From then on he tried his hardest to be more gentle and kind toward her.

Belle and the Beast began to have long talks. They took walks around the castle and played in the snow. Soon they were good friends.

Belle helped the Beast become more of a gentleman. The Beast tried to keep Belle from feeling too lonely at the castle.

"I do miss my father," Belle said one day. "I wish I could see him again."

The Beast knew that Belle truly wanted to be with her father. The Beast was Belle's friend. He wanted her to be happy. The Beast gave Belle a magic mirror. When she looked in it, she could see her father. He was sick and alone!

"Go home to your father," the Beast said. "Use the mirror to remember me."

Belle soon found Maurice in the woods. He had returned home, and had asked Gaston to help him rescue Belle. Gaston told the townspeople that Maurice must be crazy. So Maurice set off alone.

"How did you escape from the horrible beast?" Maurice asked Belle when they returned home.

"He's different now," Belle said.

Suddenly, someone pounded on the door.

"We've come to collect your father," a man told Belle, pointing to a truck from the asylum.

"He was raving about a beast," Gaston said.

"My father isn't crazy and I can prove it!" Belle showed the townspeople the Beast in the mirror.

"We're not safe!" Gaston shouted. He led the townspeople to the Beast's castle. Belle followed.

The Beast did not want to fight Gaston. When he saw Belle, his heart soared. She had come back. But when the Beast reached for Belle's hand, Gaston lashed out and wounded him.

Belle ran to the Beast. "I love you!" she cried.

Stars began to fall around them. The Beast rose into the air. His wounds healed. A light shone around him. Then the Beast turned into a prince!

Because Belle had seen his true beauty, the spell was broken!

Belle: A Tale of Kindness

Kindness means being thoughtful and helpful to others. It means taking care to be gentle with someone's feelings. It's very important to be kind, and it's also easy. Just think about how you feel when someone is nice to you or goes out of their way to be helpful. You can be just as thoughtful.

Belle was terribly lonely in the Beast's castle until the enchanted friends went out of their way to make her feel better. And even though the Beast didn't seem very kind at first, Belle took the time to get to know him and was careful with his feelings. With a little kindness, and love, Belle and the Beast were able to find enchanted happiness!

A Tale of Friendship

Once there was a sweet princess named Snow White. She sang to the wishing well to ask for her true love to find her.

That very day, a handsome prince rode onto the castle grounds. He took one look at Snow White and instantly fell in love.

But Snow White's evil stepmother, the Queen, was jealous of Snow White's beauty. Every day, the Queen asked her Magic Mirror, "Who is the fairest one of all?"

And every day, the Queen's Magic Mirror answered, "You are the fairest one, my Queen."

Then one day, unexpectedly, the Magic Mirror said something else. It said that Snow White was the fairest. It said that nothing could hide Snow White's true beauty.

The Queen was angry. She ordered her Huntsman to take Snow White into the forest and make sure she never came back. The sad Huntsman warned Snow White to hide so the Queen would never find her.

Snow White was all alone and frightened. She didn't know where to go. Soon she began to cry.

The animals of the forest heard Snow White crying and wanted to help her. They led her past a stream, down a path, and right to a little cottage.

"It's like a doll's house," Snow White said. *Knock, knock,* Snow White tapped on the door. When no one answered, she let herself in.

Inside the cottage, Snow White found seven little plates and seven little chairs. She thought that seven little children lived there because the cottage was so messy. She decided to surprise them by tidying up.

The forest animals helped Snow White clean every corner of the tiny house. They dusted, scrubbed, and swept the mess away.

When all the work was done, Snow White felt very sleepy. She went upstairs and found seven little beds all in a row. "I'll take a little nap," she said with a yawn.

When the Seven Dwarfs came home from working at the diamond mine, something seemed strange. The cottage had been cleaned! They could not believe their eyes. They heard a strange sound from upstairs and bravely tiptoed up the creaky steps to their bedroom.

Snow White was just waking up when she saw the Seven Dwarfs peering at her. "You're little men! How do you do? I'm Snow White."

Snow White explained that she had to hide from the Queen. The Dwarfs promised to help her.

Back at the castle, the Queen went to her Magic Mirror. The mirror said that Snow White was still more beautiful than she. It told her that Snow White was living in the cottage of the Seven Dwarfs.

The Queen was furious! She disguised herself as a peddler woman and made a special apple that would make Snow White sleep forever. The only thing that would wake her was Love's First Kiss.

"One taste of the apple, and her eyes will close forever," the Queen cackled.

The next morning, the Seven Dwarfs left for work. Before they went, they warned Snow White to watch out for strangers.

Snow White said good-bye to her friends and promised she would not let anyone in the cottage.

Later, there was a loud knock at the door. It was an old peddler woman, and she was selling apples. Snow White did not know that the peddler was the evil Queen, so she invited the old woman into the cottage. Then the Queen tricked Snow White into biting the poisoned apple. After just one bite of the apple, Snow White fell into a deep sleep.

The forest animals saw what happened and ran to get help from the Dwarfs. The Dwarfs hurried home as fast as they could, but they were too late. They chased the wicked Queen into the woods, and she was never seen again.

The Dwarfs were sad. They loved Snow White. She was a good friend to them. They would have done anything to save her.

The Seven Dwarfs made a bed in the forest and sat by her side every day.

The Prince heard of the sleeping girl and thought she might be Snow White. He rode his horse into the woods to find his true love.

When the Prince saw Snow White, he kissed her, and she opened her eyes! The Seven Dwarfs and the animals were overjoyed. They knew their friend's wish had finally come true!

Snow White: A Tale of Friendship

A friend is someone you enjoy spending time with. It's someone who makes you feel good about yourself. Friendship is the relationship between friends. Friendship is very important, especially in times of trouble.

Snow White was kind, gentle, and caring. Those are all good qualities to have in a friend. It's no wonder then that when Snow White was in trouble, her friends rushed to help her. Everyone from the Queen's servant to the woodland animals to the Seven Dwarfs — even Grumpy! — cared about Snow White and did all they could to help her be safe and happy. After all, that's exactly what friends are for!